THE HAPPY
ORPHELINE

THE HAPPY ORPHELINE

BY

Natalie Savage Carlson

PICTURES BY

Garth Williams

A YEARLING BOOK

Published by
DELL PUBLISHING CO., INC.
750 Third Avenue
New York, N. Y. 10017
Reprinted by arrangement with Harper & Row, Publishers, Incorporated
Printed in U.S.A.
Second Dell Printing—December 1971

For
Stephanie and Bob
Sullivan

THE HAPPY
ORPHELINE

CHAPTER ONE

Not long ago there was a little girl who lived in a village near Paris. Her first name was Brigitte and her last name didn't matter because she lived in an orphanage.

It was a big stone house surrounded by tall gray walls. It looked grim and forbidding, which just goes to show that it is the inside of things which really matters. For through the iron gate and across the cobbled courtyard was the home of twenty happy little girls. They

were *orphelines*, as the French call girl orphans. They were happy little orphelines because they were well treated. And Brigitte was the happiest of all because that was her way.

She wore her brown hair in a fat braid hanging down her back like a tassel of millet seed. And she wore tiny gold earrings that a visiting lady had once given to her. The lady had frightened Brigitte by talking about adopting her. All of the orphelines had been frightened.

"We are one big family," Brigitte had told the lady. "We want to stay together."

So the lady had bought a finch at the bird market in Paris instead of adopting a child. And Brigitte had been allowed to keep the earrings because the bird couldn't wear them.

"We are the biggest family in Ste.

Germaine," said Brigitte, "because we make twenty. Not many families have twenty children."

"I wanted twenty children when I was first married," said Madame Flattot, the woman in charge of them. "But since I never had any children of my own, working here is my second choice."

Madame Flattot was a cheerful woman whose head was crowned by a beautiful braid which she took off and laid on top of her bureau every night.

"I raise you as I would have raised my own twenty children—if I had had them," said Madame whenever she was obliged to scold the orphelines.

Genevieve, the blue-eyed girl who took care of them, was not old enough to always know how to raise twenty children the right way, so they received few scoldings from her.

"I am going to have twenty children when I get married," she told the orphelines one day, "so I am happy to be able to practice on you. Now what game shall we play? It is cold and rainy so we have to stay inside today."

Brigitte tossed her thick braid and fingered her gold earrings.

"No games now, Genevieve," she begged. "Tell us about your godmother's dog."

"Yes, Genevieve," cried Josine, the smallest orpheline of all. "Please tell us about Zezette."

Then Genevieve pretended to look annoyed although she really loved to tell about her godmother's dog.

"I have told you about Zezette a thousand times," she said.

"We want to hear a thousand more times," cried Brigitte.

"A thousand and one," added Josine, who was learning to count and wanted to show her knowledge. "A thousand and two. A thousand and three. A thousand and—"

Genevieve playfully pulled one of Josine's curls.

"All right," she gave in, "I shall tell you again. My godmother had a gray poodle named Zezette."

"And she wore her topknot in two braids hanging in front of her ears," cried Brigitte, who could never wait

4

for anything. "With blue bows on them."

Genevieve looked at her in mock surprise. "Who? My godmother?" she asked.

Then the orphelines burst into delighted laughter. Genevieve could say the funniest things.

"No, no," said Brigitte. "Zezette the poodle."

"Then let me tell about it," said Genevieve, "or you will get me all mixed up and I will say that it was my godmother who choked on a bone and died in five minutes."

"Five minutes," repeated Josine. "Six minutes, seven minutes, eight minutes."

Brigitte clapped her hand tightly over Josine's mouth. "It was Zezette who choked on the bone," she said. "Poor Zezette!"

Genevieve looked offended. "She is not poor Zezette at all," she said. "She is my godmother—oh, no, no. How you are mixing me up! It was Zezette who choked on the bone. And now she is buried in the cemetery of the dogs in Asnières."

"In a little marble tomb just like a real person," said Brigitte.

"With flowers planted at her feet," said Josine. "One geranium, two geraniums, three geraniums—"

"And her picture framed in the headstone," interrupted Brigitte, "just as if she were a real person."

"A picture of her standing on her hind legs," said Genevieve gravely, "just like when she danced the minuet for my godmother."

Josine began to look sad. "Zezette is dead," she said.

Brigitte put her arm around her. "Of course she's dead, Josine," she explained. "Dogs have to die sometime so other dogs will get their chance to be pets."

"Zezette is very happy," said Genevieve. "She is never alone because there are so many other dogs with her. So peacefully they stay together on the little island in the Seine. Never any barking or biting or growling. So unlike the wicked dogs of Ste. Germaine."

The orphelines began hopping around Genevieve like magpies.

"Oh, I wish we could go to the dog cemetery and see Zezette," cried Brigitte.

"Me, too," added Josine.

"Instead of the museums," said Yvette.

"Please, please take us to the dog cemetery, Genevieve," begged Brigitte.

"Sometime," replied Genevieve dreamily.

Then the orphelines began to beseech her even more strongly because they had learned from experience that "sometime" usually meant "never."

The noise brought Madame Flattot out of the kitchen where she had been overseeing preparations for supper.

"You shouldn't tell them such sad stories, Genevieve," she scolded.

"It isn't a sad story, Madame," cried Brigitte. "It ends so happily with the dogs staying together peacefully and no barking or biting."

"There will be barking and biting here if you children don't pick up your playthings and put them in the chest," said Madame Flattot. "I don't know who would want to adopt an untidy child."

Then a wail went up from the orphelines.

"We don't want to be adopted," cried Brigitte. "I'm glad that the lady got a bird instead of me."

"Anyone who adopted us probably wouldn't have any other children," said Yvette. "It would be so lonely."

Then Josine began to cry because she was especially afraid of being adopted—since she was the youngest and the prettiest.

"I don't want to be adopted," she sobbed. "I don't want to leave Brigitte."

"And I don't want to be adopted and taken away from Charlotte and Brigitte and Josine and all the others," blubbered Yvette.

"And I don't want to be taken away from Josine and you and Genevieve," cried Brigitte to Madame Flattot. "We don't need any more mothers. We have Madame and Genevieve and Our Blessed Mother in Heaven."

"And France," added the practical Madame Flattot. "You must remember that France is your mother because

9

she buys your food and clothing. Through Monsieur de Goupil."

Of course there was Monsieur de Goupil who was in charge of the orphanage, but he lived away in Paris. Everyone stood in awe of Monsieur because it was said that he had noble blood.

Josine began to wail louder. Brigitte hugged her.

"I won't let anyone adopt you, Josine," she promised.

"Come, come," said Madame Flattot because it went against her heart to see her children in tears. "Of course you won't be adopted by anyone because I would tell what noisy children you are. Wipe your eyes, Josine, and I will let you help me bake the Kings' Cake."

Then the orphelines were happy again.

"The Feast of the Kings is tomorrow," remembered Brigitte. "It is the day that they visited the Little Jesus in the stable."

"One king, two kings, three kings," said Josine proudly.

Then all forty eyes, magpie-bright, turned upon the crêche on the corner table. Christmas had gone by, but the crêche with its tiny clay figures of Holy Ones and villagers would stay in place until *La Chandeleur,* the day of Candlemas. Madame Flattot was very particular about that because she was from Provence, and that was the way they did things in southern France.

And tomorrow the kings and their camels would be arriving in the stable of a village where all the tiny people wore old Provençal costumes.

"Long ago the people of Provence, who molded these figures so cleverly, thought that Bethlehem was a village like their own," explained Madame Flattot, "so that is why we have the tile-roofed houses and the windmill up on the hill."

The children ran over to the crêche. They began re-arranging the twigs and pebbles that they had gathered for the scene. Josine thought the mirror pool should be placed on the other side of the village. Brigitte moved the round gypsy cart closer to the woman on the donkey so there would be room for the kings to pass with their camels.

Madame Flattot stood with her big red hands on her hips, watching them proudly. When she was first married, she had bought the crêche figures for the children she expected to have. And since they had never appeared, she had given the figures to the children that France had so generously provided.

"You had better move the kings and their camels along the road," said Madame. "Tomorrow morning they will have to arrive with their gifts."

"Did anyone bring the Little Jesus a cake?" asked Josine, who had decided that all the tiny figures needed moving.

"Of course not," said Brigitte. "He was already a King so He didn't have to find the bean in the cake."

The orphelines turned their twenty faces to Madame Flattot.

"You won't forget to put the bean in the cake, will you?" they asked her anxiously.

The bean was the most important part of the Kings' Cake on the Feast of Epiphany. Whoever found the bean in her piece of cake was queen for the rest of the day. Yvette had found the bean the year before and she was still acting queenly about it.

Little Josine settled their doubts. "If Madame lets me help make the cake," she said, "I will make sure that the bean is put in it."

Then the orphelines were truly satisfied. Madame Flattot or Genevieve might forget to put in the bean— but never Josine.

They chattered like magpies about the coming Feast of the Kings. Who would be queen this year?

They had completely forgotten Zezette.

They had also forgotten to pick up their toys. But Genevieve stealthily gathered up balls and dolls and put them into the chest. Then she looked over the big room that was so shabby and scarred because so much playing had been done in it.

"How dreadful it would be if someone did adopt one of them," she whispered to herself.

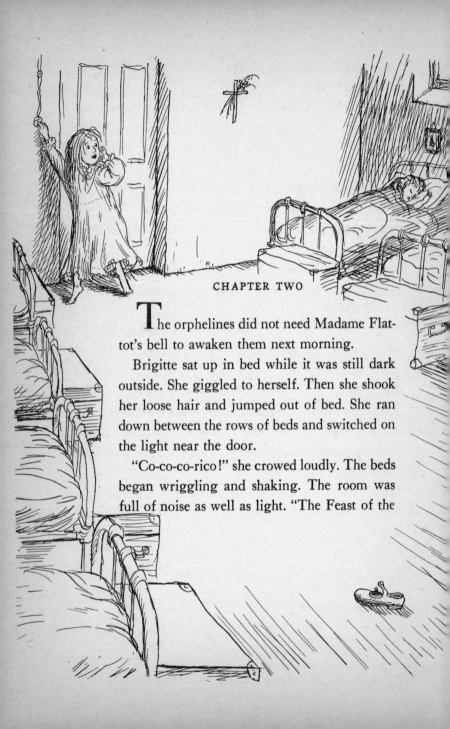

CHAPTER TWO

The orphelines did not need Madame Flattot's bell to awaken them next morning.

Brigitte sat up in bed while it was still dark
outside. She giggled to herself. Then she shook
her loose hair and jumped out of bed. She ran
down between the rows of beds and switched on
the light near the door.

"Co-co-co-rico!" she crowed loudly. The beds
began wriggling and shaking. The room was
full of noise as well as light. "The Feast of the

Kings," cried Yvette excitedly.

Josine rubbed her eyes with her chubby fists and yawned a big pink yawn. "The bean in the cake," she tried to say while her mouth was still full of the yawn.

"Time to bring the three kings to the stable," Brigitte reminded them.

They didn't wait to dress. They raced down the narrow, winding stairs in their long-sleeved nightgowns. By the time Genevieve had arrived, hastily buttoning her dressing gown, the kings had already arrived at the stable and one of the camels had fallen off the table and broken his neck.

"I will glue it back on again," promised Genevieve, "but everything in its turn. First we must dress and go to Mass in the village."

The orphelines tried to act piously and think pious thoughts as they dressed. Genevieve helped the younger ones with their hair. Brigitte brushed her own hair and braided it. Then she helped Genevieve make Josine's curls by coaxing the hair around her finger with a wet brush.

"Each one must have her own way of doing her hair," Genevieve often said. "You all dress alike so each must have a hairdress of her own so she will be herself."

What she said about dressing alike was true. Each orpheline put on a blue wool dress, her holiday best.

15

Each orpheline pulled on a blue cape and peaked hood.

Genevieve counted them as they hopped across the cobblestones which were still wet from the winter rain. "*Un, deux, trois, quatre,*" she began, because that is the way the French count and they don't think that one, two, three, four is any better.

"Oh, please let me count us," begged Josine.

"Next time," promised Genevieve. "We are in a hurry." Then she swung the gate back on its rusty hinges and the twenty orphelines burst into the village street.

"By fives we do it," said Genevieve, "holding hands so we don't lose each other."

So the children divided themselves into rows of five, one behind the other, and held hands as they marched to church. They marched down the business street, where all the buildings looked as if they had been sliced by the butcher's knife and browned in the baker's oven.

They held hands while they marched under the golden horse-heads of the horse meat shop. They held hands as they stopped to stare into the *patisserie* windows where all the rich, fancy cakes were being piled on the marble counter. They held hands as they marched past the green and white cross of the drugstore.

But they couldn't hold hands any longer when they came to the butcher's window.

"The butcher is a great artist," said Genevieve, who liked to look in his window too. Carcasses of beef hanging from the ceiling were decorated with paper rosettes. The pork sausage was shaped into a pig with truffles in its snout. But most artistic of all was the fat goose made of minced poultry with a yellow carrot for a beak.

It was hard to tear themselves away from the butcher's window. But they clasped hands again and Genevieve counted them again. They started to sing a Christmas carol, although it was really too late for that.

As they went singing down the cobbled street, they passed a woman leading a little boy by the hand. The woman looked at them and sadly shook her head.

"They are poor unhappy little orphelines," she told the boy.

Soon the business part of the village ended at the deserted market square. They crossed the square and were soon going down a quiet street bordered by high walls and tall wooden gates. Behind the walls, houses were half-hidden in small gardens. A few of the houses pretended to be castles and one of them looked more like a cuckoo clock than a building. But most of them were content to stand as square stone houses that would outlast the families they sheltered.

Although it was winter, the vines and bushes in the gardens were bright green from all the rain. Only the trees were black and bare, although some of them were leafy with big clumps of mistletoe.

A great shepherd dog lunged at its fence as the children went past. They looked at the sign on the gate. *"Chien Méchant,"* it said.

"That means 'Wicked Dog,'" Genevieve told Josine because she was too young to read.

"I don't think he is really wicked," said Brigitte, looking at the shepherd that was whining at them. "I think he is lonely and wants to take a walk with us."

On every gate was the sign saying "Wicked Dog."

"Suppose all the wicked dogs should get out and bite us," said Josine.

Genevieve smiled wryly. "I don't think you have to worry about that," she answered. "I'm sure the dogs wouldn't bite a grasshopper. I think their owners are only trying to scare robbers away."

The orphelines were indignant.

"Why don't they lock their doors instead?" asked Josine.

"What a mean thing to do," said Brigitte. "To give a nice dog a bad name! I bet your godmother didn't have a sign on the gate saying 'Wicked Dog' when Zezette was alive."

"Indeed not," replied Genevieve. "Her sign said, 'Beware of the Dog.'"

Brigitte patted the head of the next wicked dog through the pickets. He licked her hand and begged her to let him out of the gate.

"Be careful," warned Genevieve. "Some of the dogs may believe their signs."

Then a young woman with pink hair clicked past them on high heels. She gave Genevieve a make-believe smile.

"Poor little orphelines," she said. "I wish I could adopt all of them, but I really have no time for children."

Then the orphelines walked close to Genevieve all the rest of the way to church. They thought how terrible it would be if they had a mother with pink hair.

And all the time they were at Mass, they had to squeeze their eyelids and hands together to put out thoughts of wicked dogs and women who called them "poor little orphelines."

Of all of them, Josine found it hardest to think about

Heaven and God and the three kings. But she was able to think of the Kings' Cake. She was able to think up a very clever idea for helping Madame Flattot with the cake.

It was Brigitte who first noticed her clever idea. When supper was over and each orpheline had cleaned her plate with her piece of bread, Madame Flattot and Genevieve proudly carried in the Kings' Cake on a huge platter held between them. It was a round, flat piece of pastry crisscrossed with lines to mark each portion.

Since Josine was the smallest girl, it was her place to preside over the cutting of the cake and say to whom each piece should go.

"My piece looks as if someone had stuck her finger in it," said Brigitte with distaste.

"Come, come," said Madame Flattot, who was wearing her fine black velvet dress for the feast. "You

must not find fault with a cake that took me all morning to make."

"And the bean is really in it," said Josine.

Eagerly the twenty orphelines bit into their cake. *Croque, croque.* The cake was a little tough but no one mentioned that.

Suddenly Brigitte stuck her fingers into her mouth. She triumphantly pulled out half a bean. "I almost chewed it all up," she cried.

"Perhaps I should have let the baker make the cake," said Madame Flattot under her breath to Genevieve. But then she shouted loudly, "Long live the Queen! Long live Queen Brigitte!"

She took the gilt paper crown from the sideboard and set it on Brigitte's pert head, where it matched her earrings. Genevieve made a curtsey to the new Queen and ended it with a stiff-legged dance.

Brigitte was radiant with her happiness. She forgot all about the finger mark in her piece of cake.

"The Queen is happy," cried Josine.

"The Queen is smiling," said Genevieve.

"I smiled when I was queen last year," Yvette reminded them.

Games followed the dinner and of course they had to play what the Queen chose.

"I chose *cache-cache* last year," Yvette remembered.

"Maybe Brigitte would like to play it again."

"I don't want to play hide-and-seek," said Josine. "I always get found first."

Brigitte shook her head and the crown almost fell off.

"The Queen objects," said Charlotte.

"The Queen is going to speak," said Genevieve.

Brigitte spoke. "I want to play *plume-poil*," she said. "I think it is the most fun."

"The Queen orders you to play feather-fur," said Madame Flattot.

So she found an old bicycle horn and took her own bell from the sideboard.

"Josine can be 'it' first," said Brigitte. "Now in turn each of us will imitate some beast or bird. If it is a beast, Josine will ring the bell. If it is a bird, she will blow the horn. And if she makes a mistake, someone else becomes 'it.'"

"The Queen should be first," said Yvette. "I was first when I was queen."

Brigitte got down on her hands and knees, trying to balance her crown the while. "Ouaf! Ouaf!" she barked. But before Josine could sound horn or bell, Brigitte slowly rose to her feet with her wrists held together in front of her and her hands drooping. She took five slow dance steps.

"Zezette!" cried Josine, so excited that she rang the bell and tooted the horn all at the same time.

"Zezette dancing the minuet," cried Genevieve.

And so the game went on with Brigitte as "it."

Madame Flattot had other duties to perform. "Before your humble subject departs," she said to Brigitte, "give her your last command."

24

Brigitte stood up straight and raised her crowned head
high. "I command you to let Genevieve take us to the dog
cemetery next Thursday," she commanded. Thursday is
a holiday in French schools.

Madame was flustered. "But it is winter," she said. "It
will be cold and muddy there now."

"The Queen has commanded," cried the children.

Madame Flattot looked around helplessly. "The Louvre," she suggested. "Wouldn't you all like to go to the Louvre museum again and see the pretty paintings and statues?"

"No, no," cried Yvette. "The Queen commands that we go to the dog cemetery."

"Perhaps Napoleon's tomb," put in Madame Flattot. "He is buried indoors so you wouldn't get your feet wet."

"No, the dog cemetery," shouted twenty voices.

Madame Flattot was defeated. She bowed herself out of the Queen's presence. "The dog cemetery it shall be," she said as she left, but she added four threatening words, "if it doesn't rain."

The orphelines ended their Feast of the Kings by praying that Thursday would be a clear day.

"I was so lucky to be queen," sighed Brigitte as she took off her golden crown and carefully laid it on the pink chest at the foot of her bed.

Josine stood on her tiptoes and pulled Brigitte's uncrowned head down to her lips. She began to whisper in her ear.

"That really was a finger hole in your cake," she confessed. "I made it so I'd know which piece to give you."

CHAPTER THREE

The orphelines prayed so hard that God had to answer their prayers. He sprinkled the earth in the morning because He had to answer the farmers' prayers too. But He sent the sun out in all its brightness that Thursday afternoon.

Brigitte was so impatient and excited that she thought something would surely burst inside her before they ever reached the dog cemetery. Then a disappointing thought came to her.

"We have no flowers to put on Zezette's grave," she said. "There are none growing in the courtyard now."

Madame Flattot saw to it that they had flowers even though it was winter. She brought out her old summer hat and snipped off the bunch of artificial violets. "They look quite well considering that they are five years old," she assured them. "And next summer I will put a feather on my hat instead of flowers."

Josine was allowed to carry the precious violets.

Madame Flattot waved them through the big gate. "Keep together and don't play in puddles," she instructed them.

Hand in hand, the rows of happy little girls walked down the street square to catch the Asnières autobus. Genevieve followed behind, holding Josine's hand.

People who passed them on the street smiled.

"Poor little orphelines," said a woman walking out in her bedroom slippers. "How nice that they can have an outing!"

"We are going to the dog cemetery in Asnières," Josine called to her.

Then the woman frowned as if she did not approve of such an outing for poor little orphelines.

When they reached the market square, they lined up along the curb. Genevieve counted the francs in her black purse, which was really a man's tobacco pouch.

She satisfied herself that there were enough. She pushed the pouch deeply into her pocket so a pickpocket would not be able to steal it.

Three boys dressed like American cowboys were chasing each other around the posts of the market place. The most daring one ran up to the orphelines and pointed his toy pistol at them.

"Stick him up!" he ordered in English.

Brigitte pushed her hand through her cape and pointed her finger at him. "Pan! Pan! Boum!" she shouted.

"Oh, là, là! They got me!" cried the cowboy as he fell to the ground, pretending to be shot.

Then the green autobus swung around the corner and stopped in front of the children. Genevieve herded the orphelines up the back steps. *"Un, deux, trois,"* she counted as they climbed aboard.

"You said I could count us this time," Josine reminded her.

"On the way home," said Genevieve. "Hurry! This bus will be so crowded when we all get on. *Quatre, cinq, six—"*

The twenty orphelines were filling the back of the autobus. But when the conductor saw the girls in their blue cloaks and hoods, he shouted to the other passengers, "Advance! Advance and make room for the little orphelines!"

So all the people squeezed tighter together and a nice old man with a beard that covered his chest gave Josine a seat on his knees.

"I hope that you pray for your dear father and mother," said the old man.

"Oh, yes, Monsieur," put in Brigitte quickly because sometimes Josine gave the wrong answers to strangers. "Every night we pray for them and Madame Flattot and Genevieve and our mother France and Monsieur de Goupil."

"Sometimes we forget Monsieur de Goupil because he lives in Paris," added Josine because she felt that the

question rightfully belonged to her.

A woman with two children looked sadly at the girls, but when one of her own children edged toward them, she pulled him back.

"Don't get too near the orphelines, Alain," she warned. "You might catch something from them."

Genevieve heard her and the words made her blue eyes freeze up. She tried to gather her orphelines closer. "Don't get too near the lady and her children," she ordered them. "They might catch good manners from you."

But the orphelines were so interested in the scenes outside the bus that they paid little attention to what was said inside it.

They bounced up and down as the autobus rumbled over cobbles. They lurched from side to side as it lumbered around sharp corners. Sometimes the streets were so narrow they thought the bus would surely bump into the houses.

Brigitte squealed when a stout woman with seven children stepped in front of the bus so unexpectedly that the driver had to jam on the brakes. The passengers fell over each other. The woman with all the children looked at the bus for the first time. She scowled at the driver as if his bus had no right to be on the street when she wanted to take her family across it. Josine poked Brigitte excitedly.

"Is that fat woman with all the children our mother France?" she asked eagerly.

"Of course not," answered Brigitte. "France isn't one woman. We can't see her but she is all around us."

"Like God?" asked Josine.

"No, Josine," said Brigitte patiently. "God is up in heaven but France is down here on earth with us."

The autobus wove in and out of people on bicycles and people on foot. Sometimes it met other cars and once it had to pull up on the sidewalk to let another autobus pass.

Soon they were out in the country and the orphelines could look across flat fields divided into narrow strips. Men and women in old clothes and big shoes were working in the fields because many vegetables were still growing. They passed plots of green leeks and lettuce and Brussels sprouts.

A man was plowing the field for his early spring planting. The bus had to stop to let a woman get on, so all the children looked at the great gray horse with its huge hoofs and clipped tail. The man was proud that his horse was receiving so much attention. He was even a little jealous. He began masterfully shouting, *"Gioc!"* and jerking on the reins to show the people on the bus that he was superior to his horse.

Then the bus started up. It entered a long stretch of

33

woods. Some people were walking in the woods. They did
not seem to mind the dampness or the fact that the trees
were bare and the ground sodden with dead leaves. The
autobus had to keep turning into the middle of the road

to pass barelegged boys on bicycles with picnic packs
slung over their shoulders.

"Perhaps they are going to the dog cemetery too," said
Josine.

At last the autobus reached the outskirts of Asnières. It

crawled through streets that looked no different from those of Ste. Germaine. There were the same golden horse-heads over the horse butcher shops and the same green and white crosses in front of the drugstores. Even the men in their shapeless coats, padded shoes and berets looked as if they belonged to Ste. Germaine.

But when the children saw the ugly factory buildings crowding the banks of the Seine River, they thought Asnières didn't look anything like their pretty village.

As the bus neared the Clichy Bridge, Genevieve gave the children the signal to get ready to leave. The autobus stopped right across from the bridge. The children were so excited that they pushed and shoved their way out. No one they touched could possibly have caught good manners from them.

First they rushed to the bridge.

"The Seine River!" cried Yvette. "Look at all the long barges!"

The narrow, quiet river wandered lazily this way and that as if it did not care how soon it entered Paris proper. But the long boats were in a great hurry with their impatient "put-put-puts."

"That barge is carrying coal from Belgium," Genevieve pointed out. "And the one with the clotheslines on the deck is bringing stones and sand from the quarries outside Paris."

"The dog cemetery!" cried Brigitte. "There it is on that little island. I can see the tombs!"

The children streamed over the bridge to the arched gateways on the right-hand side.

"Look!" Josine pointed upward. "See the statues of dogs!"

"Just like the Louvre," cried Brigitte.

But when they came to the iron gates, they found them closed and padlocked.

"It must not be two o'clock yet," said Genevieve.

The orphelines pressed their faces between the iron bars. In front of them was a large monument with the figure of a little girl sitting on the back of a great St. Bernard dog.

"It is Barry, the dog who saved the lives of forty people lost in the Alps," explained Genevieve. "He was killed saving the forty-first."

"I wish we had a big dog like that," said Brigitte.

"I wish I could get lost in the Alps so I could ride on Barry's back," said Josine.

Some other people joined them to wait for the gate to open. A woman arrived carrying a bunch of pink hothouse roses. Josine looked from them to the violets from Madame Flattot's hat. "Our flowers will last longer," she told Genevieve. "Madame said they lasted for five years on her hat. One year, two years, three years, four years,

38

five years."

"My Toutou loved roses," the woman explained to Genevieve. "I bring them every week and I know that my Toutou wags her tail with happiness just like when she was alive."

A middle-aged gentleman came leading a spaniel. He probably wanted his dog to see what a happy end awaited those pets faithful to their masters and mistresses.

A chill breeze suddenly blew down the Seine. The orphelines drew their cloaks tighter around their shoulders and danced on their toes to keep warm. The woman with the roses covered them with their tissue paper. The man with the spaniel studied his wrist watch.

"It is exactly two o'clock," he said. "Right now the gate should open. But it is closed and no one is in sight."

"It is an outrage," declared the woman with the roses.

"The matter should be reported to the proper authorities," said another woman.

"Suppose no one ever opens the gate," cried Brigitte desperately.

"We won't get to see Zezette," wailed Josine. "We won't ever get to see Zezette."

The gentleman with the spaniel took hold of the gate and fiercely rattled it. "You should be open," he scolded the gate. "It is three minutes after two and the sign says two o'clock."

"The caretaker will surely open it soon," said Genevieve, trying to soothe her orphelines and all the impatient people. "He is probably eating a larger lunch than usual."

But the grownups were infuriated that a caretaker should eat so much in the middle of the day.

When a toothless old woman, with a giant key in her hand, finally came to unlock the gate, she explained to them that she was late because her husband was sick in bed.

"He shouldn't eat such a big lunch," said the man with the spaniel because that was fixed in his mind as the reason the gate was late in opening.

The orphelines flooded through

the gate. Genevieve stood in line to buy their tickets. "Don't go too near the bank or you might fall into the Seine," she called to them.

But none of them heard her.

Brigitte clasped her hands in ecstasy at sight of the rows of little tombs lining the paths. Some of them had pictures of the dogs framed in their headstones. Some had larger monuments shading them. There was the statue of a dog bearing the words that "Bamboule has come home to rest forever and will never be forgotten by his little mama."

Only kindly things were written on the tombs. There were no signs that said "Wicked Dog."

"Such beautiful names!" exclaimed Brigitte. "I wish I had a

name like Fifille or Poupousse or Cocolette."

"Where is Zezette?" asked Josine impatiently. "I think her name is the beautifullest."

"Here she is," cried Yvette, "with geraniums growing over her."

"No, no, she's over here," called Marie from the pathway on the other side.

"There's a Zezette behind those bushes," said Yvette, "but she's a fox terrier."

There were Zezettes all over the cemetery. The orphelines had to wait for Genevieve to lead them to the right one.

Then they clutched their hands inside their cloaks and sighed with happiness. It was Zezette's tomb exactly as they had imagined it. There was Zezette's photograph on the headstone with her gray braids. And she was standing on her hind legs.

"I bet it is more beautiful than Napoleon's tomb," said Brigitte. "Aren't you glad we came here instead of going there?"

They took turns tracing the inscription chiseled into the headstone. "You will never be forgotten, never," were the words.

"And she never will be," said Genevieve, brushing away a tear. "Not as long as my godmother and I are alive."

"I won't forget her either," promised Josine, "and I have the longest time to live because I am the youngest."

"Nor I," added Brigitte. "Not if I live to be two hundred and eleven years old."

Then Josine laid the violets from Madame Flattot's summer hat on top of the grave. Each orpheline had a turn at moving it to what she thought was a better place.

For a long time the children lingered around Zezette's cunning little tomb. Then they went exploring down paths and banks to look at the others. Some went this way toward the river. Others went that way toward the monument of a soldier with the dog that had been the mascot of his regiment during the First World War.

It was difficult for Genevieve to round them all up when it was time to leave. She made them hold hands. She counted them five times and would not trust Josine to do it. She told them that if they did not stay together, she would never bring them back and that she would leave the orphanage forever and that they would never again be treated to chocolate buns.

They took a farewell look at Zezette so gaily dancing over her own grave. Then they marched toward the arched gate.

But at sight of a tomb in a corner, Brigitte let go of Yvette's hand and ran toward it. She had overlooked this one in her exploration.

The tomb was shaped like a doghouse. On the door was written that "Our dear Riquet was the gentlest of creatures." Brigitte stood before the stone doghouse and wondered about Riquet when he had been alive. Had there been a sign of "Wicked Dog" on his gate then? Or had

45

his owner always called him the gentlest of creatures? She wanted to ask Genevieve and the others what they thought about this.

"Come here!" she called over her shoulder. Then she turned all the way around. There was not a single orpheline in sight.

Brigitte hurried to the gate. The bridge was deserted. She looked at the end of it and saw a terrible sight. There stood the green autobus and all the orphelines were getting into it. She could see Josine counting them.

"Wait!" cried Brigitte. "I make twenty."

But no one heard her. She started to run but just as she reached the end of the bridge, Genevieve stepped aboard. The conductor closed the gate and the bus lunged forward.

"Wait!" cried Brigitte desperately. "You've forgotten me."

She ran faster, but so did the bus. It reached the next block. It turned the corner.

Brigitte looked around in loneliness and fright. It was beginning to grow dark because night comes early to the Paris area in winter. The breeze was colder than ever. She was all alone in Asnières.

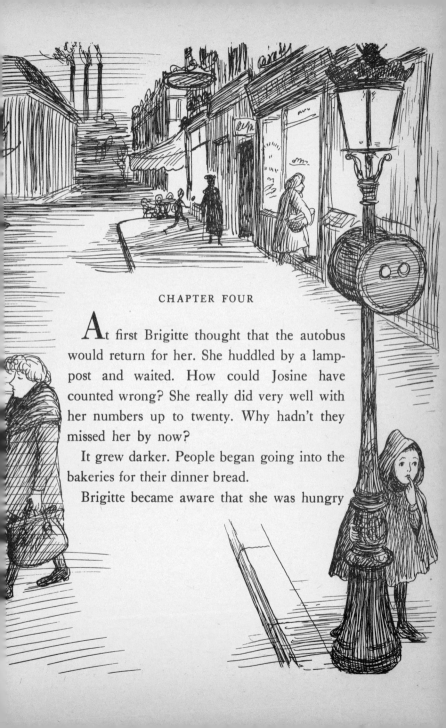

CHAPTER FOUR

At first Brigitte thought that the autobus
would return for her. She huddled by a lamp-
post and waited. How could Josine have
counted wrong? She really did very well with
her numbers up to twenty. Why hadn't they
missed her by now?

It grew darker. People began going into the
bakeries for their dinner bread.

Brigitte became aware that she was hungry

too. She thought of all the orphelines gathering around the little tables in their cheery dining room. She could almost smell the soup and ragout in the big steaming pots.

She began to wander forlornly through the streets, which were filling with people returning to their homes from their daily work in Paris or the nearby factories. Soon she was lost as well as forgotten. She would have to do something.

"Please, Madame—" she began timidly, walking up to a woman carrying a bag full of fresh vegetables. But the woman walked on without paying any attention to her.

She tried to stop a kindly looking man, but he thrust a fifty-franc coin into her hand and kept on going.

Two children were coming out of a bakery, carrying long loaves of bread. They were quarreling noisily.

"Can you help me?" Brigitte asked

one of them. But even as she spoke, one of the children raised her long loaf of bread and clubbed the other over the shoulders. The other child struck back with his own loaf. Soon chunks of bread were flying through the air. Brigitte hastily retreated.

She tried to stop some more people, but everyone seemed anxious to get to where he was going.

Then a bright idea popped up under the child's blue hood. There was one way to get attention from these people.

She stood in the middle of the sidewalk and began thinking of all the sad things she could. She didn't have to think very hard because she was already lost and cold and hungry.

Tears streamed down her face. She raised her voice in a quavering whine.

"I am a poor little orpheline," she wailed as loud as she could. "A poor lost little orpheline."

A woman stopped and stared at her. Then some others stopped.

"She is a poor little orpheline," clucked the woman sympathetically.

"I have no mama or papa," wailed Brigitte, finding that she could shout even louder.

Soon she was surrounded by a sympathetic group.

"A poor little orpheline with no mother or father," said

a woman in a shaggy fur coat.

"She is lost," explained another.

"A little lost orpheline," echoed yet another.

More people stopped to look at Brigitte.

"Someone should do something," said a woman, making no move to do anything herself.

"Call a policeman," ordered a gentleman on the fringe of the crowd.

Then an old woman carrying a cane marched to the group. She was a queer old woman with a frowsy velvet bonnet that looked like a lampshade and a furpiece that looked like an animal hide hung on her shoulders to cure.

"What is the trouble?" she asked sternly.

She had such a commanding air that the crowd respectfully drew out of her way.

"It is Madame Capet," whispered one man to his neighbor. "Her husband is a pretender to the throne of France."

They all tried at once to tell Madame Capet that a poor little orpheline was lost.

"I'm a poor, unhappy orpheline," cried Brigitte at the top of her voice. "I'll never get back to my home."

"Nonsense," said Madame Capet. "Everything will be all right because I am now in charge." She seized Brigitte's cold hand in her own skinny claws. "Come with me," she said. Then she glared at the people around

them. "Have you no dinners to get or marketing to do?" she asked crossly. "Do you think this is the May Fair in Paris?"

The people sheepishly began drifting away. Brigitte was left alone with the queer old woman. "Come, child," she commanded imperiously. "Come with me to my apartment and I shall solve your problems for you."

She led Brigitte with one hand and stamped her cane along with the other.

"Where is your orphanage?" she asked. "In Paris?"

"No, Madame," said Brigitte, drying her tears on the corner of her cape. "It is in Ste. Germaine."

"Surely not Monsieur de Goupil's responsibility?" exclaimed Madame Capet.

"Yes, Madame," answered Brigitte in surprise. She didn't know what "responsibility" meant, but Monsieur de Goupil's name was quite familiar to her ears.

"Then what are you doing in Asnières all by yourself?" asked Madame. "Did you run away?"

"Oh, no," said Brigitte. "I would never run away from the orphanage. We all came to Asnières to see the dog cemetery."

"Dog cemetery!" snorted Madame Capet. "Pouf! What a place to take children! Why not the Louvre?"

"We've been to the Louvre," said Brigitte, "but we didn't like it because they wouldn't let us touch anything.

A guard followed us all the time."

"Then the Eiffel Tower," said Madame. "You should have been taken to the top of it to look down on Paris."

"No, no, Madame," said Brigitte. "I get dizzy when I'm up high. And one time Josine fell out of the pear tree and broke her arm."

The old woman jabbed a wall viciously with her cane. "Stop calling me 'Madame,'" she ordered. "From now on you shall address me as 'Your Majesty' because I am really the Queen of France."

Brigitte grinned. "Did you find the bean in the cake too?" she asked. "I was Queen of the Epiphany this year."

"What a quaint child you are," said Her Majesty. "But here is my apartment house."

Brigitte saw a dreary stone building squeezed between factories. A broken

gate gaped at them. Madame the Queen pushed the gate with her cane and it groaned wider.

"It is not the palace of Versailles," she apologized, "but I rule here. All the tenants obey me."

She opened a doorway to a dark hall. "Don't fall over the brooms," she warned. Brigitte went ahead of her. "And be careful on the steps. Louis will have to do something about this light. It never works."

"Yes, Mad—Your Majesty," said Brigitte, then she fell over a broom and bruised herself on the steps.

"I shall reprimand the janitor about those brooms," said Madame Capet. "They have no right to be in the hallway."

Slowly Brigitte felt her way up the stairs. She went up, up until Madame pulled at her cape.

"Here we are," she said.

Brigitte could hear a key grinding. Then a door was flung open. A light was snapped on.

"As I said," repeated Madame Capet, "it is not the palace of Versailles but it is just as old."

Madame Capet did not have to say this. The apartment looked like the attic of a museum to Brigitte. The dust of centuries covered the faded velvet drapes, the cracked mirror and the ragged carpet. A head of Apollo with the nose broken off stood on a crippled table.

There was a water-stained print of Louis XIV in all

his curls hanging over the blackened coal grate. And in the very middle of the floor sat a chair of tarnished gilt with two grimy cupids trying to hold up the back.

Scarcely had the child pulled herself out of her cloak than Madame Capet thrust a broom into her hand.

"The room needs cleaning," she said. "Let me see how well Monsieur de Goupil raises his children."

Brigitte enjoyed fighting the room with the broom. She even beat the heavy curtains and made the dust fly over Louis XIV's curls. She swept all the dirt into a dustpan. She marveled that such a small room could be the home for so much dirt and rubbish.

Meanwhile Madame Capet took off her velvet bonnet and animal hide as if she were divesting herself of crown and mantle. Then the old woman, who thought herself a queen, sat down on the gilt chair as if it were a throne.

"What is your name?" she asked Brigitte.

"My first name is Brigitte," said the child, "and my last name doesn't matter because I am an orpheline."

The old lady leaned forward. "Pouf! Last names matter a great deal," she disagreed. "If Louis' name had not been Capet, I never would have learned that he is the descendant of the lost dauphin of France."

Brigitte stopped cleaning. She tried to remember her history.

"Wasn't that Marie Antoinette's little boy who was

taken away from her during the Revolution?" she asked, proud that she could remember so much.

"The same dauphin," said Madame, pleased with Brigitte's knowledge. "The French people lost him, but I found him in Louis' old trunk soon after we were married."

"Was he dead?" asked Brigitte with real interest.

"Don't be simple, child," said Madame Capet. "I found his *name* in the papers of my husband's family. Louis Capet, my husband's ancestor. Who else could be Louis Capet but the lost dauphin?"

Brigitte had no answer to this question. But Madame had more to say on the subject. "There are others who call themselves the rightful king of France," she went on, "but they are only pretenders."

Brigitte stood staring at the old woman. Somehow she had never imagined a queen looking like Madame Capet.

The royal lady pointed to an alcove hidden by an ancient silk screen. "And now you may clean up the dishes," she said. "You will have to heat water first."

Brigitte went behind the screen and found a sink full of dirty dishes. She wondered how the dishes got dirty because she couldn't see any food anywhere. And she was very hungry.

As she dried the last chipped dish, she heard someone stumble over the brooms in the dark hall.

"Hist!" called Madame Capet from her throne. "The King is approaching. You must curtsey to him. It will make him so happy because he has few loyal subjects nowadays. Even Monsieur de Goupil calls him a pretender."

Brigitte hastily hung the wet dishcloth on a nail. She went to the door. She took hold of the hem of her woolen skirt on each side. She felt as if she were acting in a play and did not want to miss her cue.

The door opened and the King entered. Only he did not look like a king either. He was a tired-looking old man in a black beret and a blue apron. At sight of Brigitte and the neat room, he began to back out.

"Pardon," he said. "I have opened the wrong door."

But the Queen rose to meet him. She also made a deep curtsey, although she had trouble rising from the floor.

"Good evening, Your Majesty," she greeted him. "And how did you find our subjects today?"

"Very, very annoying," answered the King, assured now that he was in the right apartment. "The foreman says I am getting too old to work in a factory." Then he looked at Brigitte again. "Is this one of the tenants' children?" he asked.

"No," smiled the old Queen. "She is my new little helper and I am quite satisfied with her work. I have decided that we shall adopt her."

Brigitte stiffened and her face whitened.

"No, no," she cried. "I don't want to be adopted!"

"I thought you were looking for an older girl," said the King. "This one does not look very strong."

"But she is an orpheline," put in the Queen. "One of Monsieur de Goupil's orphelines. Pouf! That will make it easier."

Brigitte felt as if she had been kidnapped. Terror froze every part of her but her tongue.

"I don't want to be adopted," she cried. "I want to go home."

Madame Capet narrowed her wrinkled eyelids. "How would you like to be a countess?" she asked. "Louis could make you one, couldn't you, Your Majesty?"

"If you really think she is strong enough for the work," agreed the old man.

"No, no," cried Brigitte. "I don't want to be a countess. I just want to be an orpheline. I'm really a very happy orpheline. I only said I was unhappy so someone would help me."

"Perhaps it would be better to hire a girl," suggested the King.

"Don't be stupid, Louis," snapped the Queen. "We would have to pay a maid-of-all-work."

Brigitte grabbed her cloak and hood. She put them on so fast they were inside out. But she didn't care.

"I'm going home," she cried desperately.

"There, there," Madame Capet tried to soothe her. "Of course you are going back to the orphanage. I will take you to Ste. Germaine on my bicycle right now. I am just learning to drive it with a motor so I need the practice."

Brigitte felt a little better. She waited for Madame to don the animal hide and the worn velvet bonnet again. She even made a polite curtsey to Louis, King of France. Then she stumbled down the dark hallway ahead of the Queen of France and fell over the brooms again.

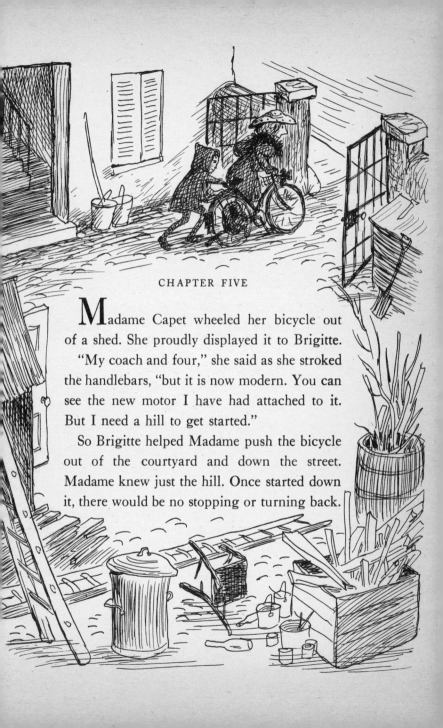

CHAPTER FIVE

Madame Capet wheeled her bicycle out of a shed. She proudly displayed it to Brigitte.

"My coach and four," she said as she stroked the handlebars, "but it is now modern. You can see the new motor I have had attached to it. But I need a hill to get started."

So Brigitte helped Madame push the bicycle out of the courtyard and down the street. Madame knew just the hill. Once started down it, there would be no stopping or turning back.

It was paved with cobblestones and its narrow street dipped to a blind intersection.

The old woman stopped under a street light and braced the bicycle against the curb. Brigitte straddled the market basket fastened behind the seat. Madame gave the bicycle a push then leaped onto the pedals like a strong youth.

"Allez!" cried Madame Capet. "We are off to Ste. Germaine."

The bicycle started down the hill. It went faster and faster over the bumpy cobblestones. Brigitte's hood fell back over her shoulders and her braid flew out behind her like the tail of a racing horse. She grabbed the seat but Madame sat down on her fingers so hard that she let go and clung to the basket instead.

Madame Capet kicked the lever beside the pedal. The motor coughed a few times then roared steadily. The bicycle went faster and faster. It almost hit a car at the intersection so Madame swiftly turned it into the path of a motorcycle. The man on the motorcycle had to jump to the ground in order to stop in time.

People who started to cross the streets quickly changed their minds. Other motorists changed their minds about where they were going too. Brigitte and the Queen overtook other bicycles and Madame passed them on the right or left, according to her whim.

"Allez!" cried Madame Capet gaily. "We will show

them who owns the roads tonight."

She said this because night was upon them. Already most of the cars and bicycles had turned on their lights. The beams of a truck nearly blinded Brigitte as Madame cut across its path.

"The right of way belongs to the Queen of France," cried Madame. So she took it from all the cars and bicycles at the next intersection. Brigitte fearfully looked over her shoulder as they missed another truck by a few inches. The driver was shouting and shaking his fist at them.

"D-do you know how to stop your bicycle?" Brigitte asked between chattering teeth.

"Pouf! Let the others know how to stop," cried Madame Capet.

They raced under the bright street lights. A young man with a helmet on his head tried to pass them on his motorcycle. Madame ended that by skidding her bicycle directly in front of him.

At one busy corner a policeman in white hat and gloves was directing traffic. He held up his white hand as a signal for Madame's bicycle to stop. Then he leaped aside just in time to save himself from being knocked down. His shrill whistle split the air.

"I think he wants us to stop," cried the orpheline against the wind.

"Pouf!" shouted Madame Capet. "Once on my bicycle I stop for no one. Ha! Look at that big American car coming around the corner. The Americans think that they own the whole world."

Straight toward the car buzzed the French bicycle. Brigitte shut her eyes and started praying as fast as she could. She heard the screeching of brakes and the squealing of tires. She opened her eyes just in time to see the American car run into a tree to get out of Madame's way.

"Crazy American driver," snorted Madame. "Now he will know that he is in France."

The bicycle reached the country road in no time. Everything was dark and shadowy except when the lights of another bicycle or car passed them.

"Can you see the edges of the road, child?" asked Madame. "I can't."

Brigitte strained her eyes.

"Stop!" she cried. "There's a red lantern ahead."

Madame's bicycle knocked the lantern down. Then it trembled and shook as it rode over loose stones. It bounced so high over a pothole that Brigitte would have fallen off except for her death grip on the basket.

"Ouf!" shouted Madame angrily. "Such a place to hang a lantern!"

They entered the woods at top speed.

"Tell me if I come too close to the trees," cried Madame. "I don't know if we are still on the road or not."

Brigitte was so terrified that she didn't know whether they were on the road or flying over the trees. She said her prayers all over again then made up some new ones of her own.

She did not think she would ever see the other children or Madame Flattot or Genevieve again. She thought that she was more likely to see the spirits of the little dogs in the cemetery.

But God answered her prayer again. He brought the bicycle safely to the gate of the orphanage at Ste. Germaine. But He allowed Madame to stop the bicycle so suddenly that Brigitte fell off into the gutter.

"You see that I can stop it," said Madame Capet triumphantly.

Brigitte picked herself up. She wanted to get away from the Queen of France as fast as possible. She hoped she would not want to come inside.

"I must go now, Madame," she gasped, making half a curtsey. "They are waiting for me. Thank you and goodbye."

Madame was bending over the handlebars of her bicycle. "How stupid of me!" she exclaimed. "I have driven all the way here without my light turned on."

She switched on the light and started the angry motor. Then she said the awful words, "I will be back next Tuesday morning."

Brigitte ran through the open gate. But she closed it behind her and drew all the bolts. She wished it could stay bolted forever.

The night light was burning in the courtyard and it looked as if every light in the house was on too. Never had the orphanage looked so warm and bright to the little orpheline.

She tugged at the big door, then ran down the hall. At sound of the footsteps, Madame Flattot flung the farther door open.

"My precious little one," she cried, squeezing Brigitte in her big soft arms.

Genevieve hugged her too. "Oh, it was all my fault,"

she cried. "All my fault! I am not fit to raise children."

Then all the orphelines came running and Brigitte could see that some of them had been weeping. Josine's cheeks were still wet.

"I didn't mean to forget you, Brigitte," she tried to explain. "I was so busy counting that I couldn't see you weren't there. And then I counted Genevieve too. That's where I made my mistake."

"Where have you been?" asked Yvette. "When you let go of my hand I thought you had gone back with Genevieve."

"How did you get home?" asked Marie. "The bus was so crowded that we didn't know you weren't on it."

No one gave her a chance to answer the questions.

"We called the police and they are still looking for you," said Genevieve.

"I even had to telephone to Monsieur de Goupil," said Madame Flattot, "and you know he does not like to be called away from his dinner."

"I will telephone him right away and tell him the little lost one is found," said Genevieve.

"And call the police," added Madame Flattot. "Already they have brought three wrong children here. Even a boy too little to know his own name."

Brigitte had never been so happy in her life. She felt surrounded by light and warmth and love. It was like a wall protecting her from all danger. She could not imagine a happier home nor kinder mothers and sisters.

"What happened to you, Brigitte?" asked Josine. "Was it exciting?"

"Do tell us, Brigitte," begged Yvette.

Brigitte looked into their eager, glowing eyes. Then she fingered her earrings airily.

"A beautiful queen found me," she began. "She wore a golden crown and her robes were of silk and ermine."

"How did she know you belonged here?" asked Josine.

"She didn't," said Brigitte, "so first she took me to her palace. It was the loveliest palace. There were great gardens fulls of fountains and statues. And inside the palace was golden furniture and velvet curtains and floors that shone like mirrors."

"Was the King there?" asked Yvette.

"Yes," said Brigitte dreamily. "He had long curls and

his clothes were of satin and lace. I curtsied to him so he said that he is going to make me a countess."

"A real countess!" gasped Yvette.

"Oh, I wish you had told him about me," said Josine wistfully.

"I did, Josine," said Brigitte quickly. "I told him what pretty curls you have and how well you can count to twenty." She suddenly reached into her pocket. "See! He gave me a fifty-franc piece and told me to buy you some chocolate buns."

Josine's eyes grew round as the coin. The others stared at it as if they had never seen the same coins in Genevieve's black tobacco pouch. Everyone had to take a turn feeling it.

"And the Queen said that she is coming back to take us all for a ride in her golden coach drawn by four white horses," continued Brigitte. "That's the way she brought me here."

"In a coach with *four* horses!" exclaimed Josine. "Oh, I wish I had been looking out of the window."

"If you had," said Brigitte, "you would have seen the fastest horses in the world. They were faster than the wind."

Madame Flattot broke in at last.

"That is enough talking," she said. "Brigitte must be tired and hungry."

"Oh, no," said Brigitte. "The Queen fed me strawberries and cream and chocolate buns. But I could still eat a bowl of soup and a piece of bread and a glass of milk and anything that's left from supper."

Madame Flattot found all these things for Brigitte and they tasted even better to the child than strawberries and cream and chocolate buns.

And when she went to bed that night, the long room with the rows of beds and chests looked grander to her than a palace full of gold furniture and velvet curtains.

Madame Flattot was glad to go to bed too. She took off her beautiful braid and laid it on her bureau. Then she turned to Genevieve, who had come to have a talk with her.

"Do you think we should allow the child to tell such stories?" asked Genevieve anxiously. "Brigitte has always had a good imagination but this is the first time she has been so untruthful."

"Nonsense!" mumbled Madame Flattot, her mouth full of hairpins. "It is good for children to use their imaginations. They get enough truth in their schoolbooks. But I wonder how the child really did get back from Asnières."

73

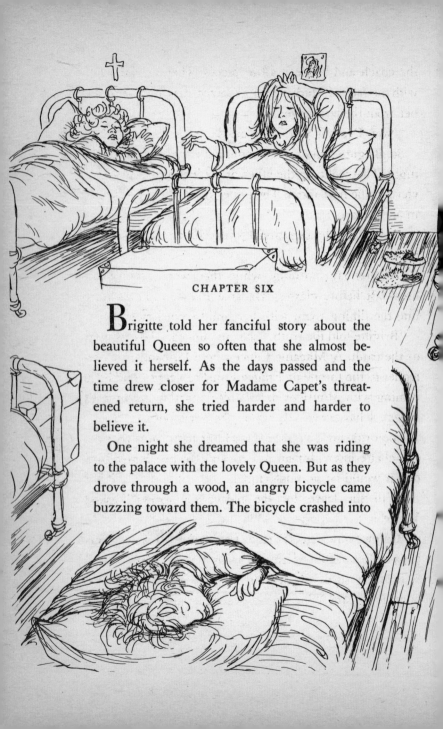

CHAPTER SIX

Brigitte told her fanciful story about the beautiful Queen so often that she almost believed it herself. As the days passed and the time drew closer for Madame Capet's threatened return, she tried harder and harder to believe it.

One night she dreamed that she was riding to the palace with the lovely Queen. But as they drove through a wood, an angry bicycle came buzzing toward them. The bicycle crashed into the coach and broke it all to pieces. Then an old witch with the face of Madame Capet seized Brigitte and pulled her from the wreckage.

"Now I've got you!" she cried.

So Brigitte woke up screaming in the middle of the night. That woke up the other orphelines and even Genevieve in the next room. The upper floor of the house was in an uproar.

"I dreamed the beautiful Queen couldn't find us," explained Brigitte.

On Monday morning, while they were eating their breakfast before classes, Madame Flattot came rushing into the dining room with her braid turned sideways.

"Brigitte told the truth," she announced. "That is, part of the truth. A Madame Capet whose husband is a pretender to the throne of France wants to adopt her. She is coming with Monsieur de Goupil tomorrow morning at eleven. I have been talking on the telephone."

The orphelines stopped munching their buns and began chattering with their mouths full. To be adopted by a queen would be no misfortune.

"Will she leave for the palace tomorrow?" asked Yvette.

"Can we go to see her real often?" asked Josine. "Perhaps the beautiful Queen will want me too."

To their surprise, Brigitte screwed up her face and burst into tears. "She isn't a beautiful queen," wept the orpheline. "She's an old witch. And she doesn't live in a palace. She lives in an old broken place full of broomsticks."

Madame Flattot was upset. "But Monsieur de Goupil says she has a good character and that she is fond of you," she persisted.

Brigitte wept into her napkin. "She made me clean up all the dirt and she didn't give me anything to eat," she sobbed. "Then her husband came—the King—and he said she should get a stronger girl to do her work."

The orphelines had a hard time to get used to this new story of Brigitte's adventure in Asnières.

"But you said he was going to make you a countess," Yvette reminded her.

"They just want me for a drudge," wailed Brigitte.

"Will you have to shine the golden coach?" asked Josine.

"There wasn't any golden coach," confessed Brigitte. "It was a rickety bicycle with a motor on it. And she drove like she was crazy and nearly killed us. All the cars were honking. And she wouldn't even stop when the policeman whistled at us."

Josine still had a hard time understanding this change in the story because she was so little.

"But the King gave you money to buy me chocolate buns," she reminded Brigitte.

"It wasn't the King," confessed the older child. "It was a man on the street who thought I was a beggar."

She wiped her eyes on the napkin and looked at the other orphelines. Their eyes were big and bright and Josine's mouth was wide open. Since Brigitte was obliged to change her story, she wanted to make the new one interesting too.

"We ran over a dozen people," she added, her own blue eyes brightening, "and all the policemen were chasing us."

But this did not change the truth of Madame Capet's imminent arrival. Madame Flattot was desolated. "What can we do?" she asked Genevieve. "How can we prevent this tragedy? Brigitte is like my own child."

"I feel the same way about her," said Genevieve. "Perhaps we could hide her in the attic."

77

Madame Flattot clucked. "You are getting as fanciful as the child, Genevieve," she said. "I will have a talk with Monsieur de Goupil, but I doubt that it will do any good. He feels that getting an orphan adopted will save money for the taxpayers."

None of the orphelines could study that morning. They tried to sit primly in their blue and white plaid aprons. But they fidgeted and squirmed and whispered to each other behind their hands.

Only Josine was her usual self. Since she was too young to study lessons, she was allowed to draw pictures on the blackboard. This morning she was busy drawing the picture of an automobile with all four of its wheels on the same side. The other orphelines began to giggle. The giggles seemed to loosen up their tight insides.

Mademoiselle Grignon, who came to teach them, was quite annoyed.

78

"You are very inattentive today," she said, "especially you, Brigitte. Aren't you interested in learning the glorious history of our France?"

Then Brigitte stopped giggling and began crying because sometimes giggles are so close to tears.

"I wish there wasn't any history," she sobbed. "I wish there wasn't any France or kings and queens."

Mademoiselle was shocked. So all the children began explaining why Brigitte didn't like history or kings or queens. Mademoiselle was even more shocked because she was a strong republican, which means she didn't believe there should be kings and queens anywhere but in history books.

"France has no king and queen any more," she said. "We are now a republic with a president and a chamber of deputies elected by the people. Madame Capet is no more a queen than I."

Brigitte dried her eyes and tried to study. But her mind wouldn't stay on her history. It began thinking of ways to escape from the Capets.

All that afternoon, instead of playing games, the orphelines tried to help Brigitte think of ways to keep from being adopted.

"Perhaps I could run away," said Brigitte.

"And leave us behind?" cried Josine.

"They would find you," said Yvette. "All the policemen know what you look like because Madame Flattot told them when you were lost in Asnières."

"If you run away, you aren't much better off than if you were with the Capets," said Marie.

Brigitte stared and stared into her wet handkerchief. She rolled it into a tight ball for the twentieth time. She was beginning to think of something worth while.

"Perhaps if I did something bad enough," she said, "the Capets wouldn't want me."

"You could throw all your clothes over the wall," said Yvette.

"Or put salt in the sugar," said Marie.

"Or cut off your hair," put in Josine, who had once done that herself.

But Brigitte shook her head to these ideas. "No," she said. "They aren't bad enough. I will have to do something terrible."

The orphelines began to be frightened. "What could you do that would be worse?" asked Yvette.

Brigitte tossed her braid and clenched her fists. "I shall let all the wicked dogs in Ste. Germaine loose," she announced.

The orphelines gasped and looked around fearfully to see that neither Madame Flattot nor Genevieve was within earshot.

"Oh, Brigitte, would you really?" asked Josine.

"Wait and see," promised Brigitte.

But next morning found Brigitte in Mademoiselle's classroom again. She had meant to leave the orphanage after breakfast to go out into the village and let the wicked dogs loose. But planning such a wicked thing was easier than actually doing it.

She looked at the clock above the blackboard. It was almost ten o'clock. Madame Capet would arrive in an hour.

Brigitte raised her hand. "May I get a drink of water?" she asked Mademoiselle. "I ate something salty for breakfast."

"Yes," nodded Mademoiselle Grignon, "but don't be long. We are going to recite our geography lesson in a few minutes."

Brigitte slid out of her seat. All the orphelines turned to watch her leave. She did not go to the kitchen to get a drink. She went to the cloakroom and pulled her blue cape and hood from the peg. She put them on and tiptoed out the oaken door. She tripped lightly over the cobblestones. She opened the big gate then slowly closed it behind her.

As she started down the street, her courage wavered. Everything looked the same as usual. There were the signs of the druggist and the horse butcher. There were the soberly dressed men and women going about their business. The street cleaners had turned on the water and were sweeping out the gutters with their twig brooms. The butcher was arranging a calf's head so artistically that it looked like a marble statue. None of those people knew that within the next hour all the wicked dogs of Ste. Germaine would be loose in the streets.

The market square was crowded and noisy because Tuesday was a market day in the village. Women with string baskets and straw baskets and baskets on wheels were headed for the square. Rows of tables had been set up under the crimped tin roofs and everything from fish and butter to safety pins and live turtles was being offered for sale. People were buying snails and brushes and pigs' noses with no idea that very soon now they would be surrounded by all the wicked dogs of the village.

Brigitte wandered among them trying to put off the awful time when she must commit her crime.

She stopped at a fish stand. She saw a basket filled with strange objects that looked like chestnut burrs. She fingered them to see if they felt as prickly as they looked. The man who was slicing a slippery fish with a long sharp knife frowned at her.

"Don't handle the sea food, little one," he said, "unless your mother has sent you to buy some."

Brigitte quickly moved away. She pushed her way through the shoppers and stopped in front of a farm

woman's stall. She thought about the terrible thing she must do before she returned to the orphanage.

"Don't stand in front of my cabbages, little girl," said the farm woman. "What housewife will buy cabbages that she cannot see?"

So Brigitte slowly walked away until she came to a man who was selling aprons. He stopped her as she went by.

"A nice apron for your mama?" he wheedled. Then he put an apron on himself and tied it in back to show her how nice her mama would look in it.

"I have no mama," said Brigitte. "I—I mean I have many mamas." Then because she knew her explanation sounded silly, she blushed and darted away.

She went to the sidewalk where the market trucks were parked and fearfully looked across the street to the houses where the wicked dogs lived.

Then a woman with a scarf over her head bumped her four-wheeled market cart into Brigitte's knees. "Why aren't you in school instead of in the way?" chided the woman.

So Brigitte had to leave the market place and do the terrible deed. The streets with the houses and gardens were quiet and deserted. It was such a nice day that bedding was hanging to air from many upper-story windows while the housewives went to market.

Brigitte was surprised to find the first gate unbolted. She looked at the sign "Wicked Dog." Then she looked through the slats at the shaggy dog lying in a patch of sunlight. She opened the gate and whistled to the dog. He came bounding out. He wagged his tail and frisked about playfully.

The next gate couldn't be opened because it was locked. And so was the next. But the third one was only bolted, so Brigitte reached through the bars and opened it. The police dog who ran out barked at Brigitte fiercely, then ran off to romp with the shaggy dog.

Many gates couldn't be opened, but most of them were only bolted by housewives in a hurry to get to market before the freshest goods were bought by others.

Soon the street was alive with dogs. There were big dogs and little dogs, short-haired dogs and long-haired dogs, and prick-eared dogs and rat-tailed dogs. Dogs with dish faces and dogs with goose rumps. Fiddle-fronted dogs and butterfly dogs.

They played together and quarreled together and barked with delight. Then Brigitte noticed some of the dogs sniffing the air. They were sniffing at the breeze that came from the market place.

"Ouaf! Ouaf!" barked the dogs happily. They ran off in the direction of the market place. All the dogs went that way. They barked and capered and growled as they raced down the street to the smell of the Tuesday market.

Brigitte put her hands to her heart to see if it was still beating. She felt as if she had done the worst thing in the world. She had let so many of the wicked dogs loose and they were all on their way to the market place.

CHAPTER SEVEN

Brigitte pulled her cloak tightly around her. It would do no good to run back to the orphanage now. The people must know who had done this fearful deed so that Madame Capet and Monsieur de Goupil would hear about it.

But when she saw the disorder at the market, she was tempted to take to her heels and run away forever.

The people were shouting and milling around. The dogs were racing from stall to stall, barking and yapping at such unknown freedom.

One of them jumped up on a butcher's table and grabbed an Alsatian sausage. Another dog tried to take it away from him. Yet others decided to get their own meat. The market place was in an uproar.

"Robbers have done it," cried a woman with a black shawl over her head. "They have let our dogs out so they can rob our houses while we are at market."

"Police! Police!" shouted the meat man.

"Police!" shouted the woman with the basket on wheels as one of the dogs pulled her fresh sheep's tongue from it. "Help! Fire! Murder!"

A policeman came dashing up on his bicycle. He raised his white club threateningly.

"Everyone stand still!" he shouted. "No stampeding, please!"

The people obeyed him but the dogs didn't. He started to hit one of the dogs but a strong woman grabbed his arm. "Don't you dare!" she shouted. "That's my Dodo."

Brigitte gathered her last bit of courage together. She walked up to the policeman. She tugged at his belt.

"I-it wasn't robbers who let the dogs out," she confessed. "I-I did it."

Then the outraged people crowded around her.

"The wicked child," said a West Indian woman with her hair bound up in a colored bandanna. "She should be put in jail."

"What are her parents thinking about that they don't watch her?" demanded a farm woman.

The fish man waved his knife. "She should be punished severely," he stated.

The policeman grabbed a fistful of Brigitte's cloak. He pushed back her hood and looked at her thick braid and her gold earrings. "Ha!" he exclaimed. "This must be the child who ran away in Asnières. As if I don't have enough trouble trying to find my own children when I want them!"

Brigitte looked at the man's determined face. Then she looked at the angry faces of the market people. She was terrified by what she had done. She wanted to save herself as best she could. There was only one way. She burst into frightened tears.

"I am a poor little orpheline," she howled above the barking and snarling of the dogs. "I have no papa or mama."

There was a sudden quiet among the people. Only those on the outskirts of the tight crowd were still yelling. Those close to Brigitte began to murmur. Their voices grew louder.

"She is a poor little orpheline."

"She has no parents to teach her better."

Brigitte bawled louder. "No mama or papa," she wailed again. "They died before I was born."

"Poor orpheline! She can't even remember her parents. They died when she was so young."

Their voices grew louder and shriller.

"Why is this little orpheline being treated so badly?" asked a woman carrying a bunch of celery.

"It is the policeman," answered the woman who sold cheeses. "He is arresting the poor orpheline."

Then some of the market people furiously turned upon the policeman, whom they usually treated with great respect.

"Fie upon you!" cried a truck driver. "Is this the way a great, strong man like you keeps the peace?"

"You arrest children and do nothing about the robbers who let our dogs loose," said the woman with the black shawl, because she hadn't heard everything.

And things might have gone badly for the policeman if a new disturbance had not attracted the people.

For an old woman pushed her bicycle through the crowd in an imperious manner. She was followed by Monsieur de Goupil, the manager of the orphanage.

"Take your hands off that child," Madame Capet ordered the policeman. "She is mine."

"We heard that she was in trouble," apologized Monsieur de Goupil. "The other children told us that she was planning to let all the dogs out of their gardens."

"She shall be severely punished," added Madame Capet. "I can promise you I will see to it myself because I am going to adopt her. I am the rightful Queen of France, you know." She took hold of Brigitte's quivering shoulder and shook it. "Come with me, naughty child," she ordered.

Brigitte pulled away. Then she shouted louder than ever. "I don't want to be adopted by you," she cried. "I don't want to be adopted by anyone. That's why I let the wicked dogs loose."

Then the people turned their anger upon Monsieur de Goupil and the Queen of France.

"How dare you adopt a child who doesn't want you for a mother?" the woman with the basket on wheels demanded of Madame Capet. She contemptuously bumped the Queen's bicycle with her basket. They all pressed closer to Madame Capet. The fish man shook his scaly fist under the royal nose. Others began hurling insults.

"No rioting!" cried the policeman. "There will be no rioting." And he hoped that he was telling the truth.

The Queen of France trembled and began backing her bicycle. "The mob," she shuddered. "It is the mob again."

"Courage, Madame," said Monsieur de Goupil, who was fast losing his own. He addressed himself to the

people. "We must find good homes for the orphans when possible," he explained. "Supporting them is a burden on the taxpayers."

The people turned from the Queen to him.

"Taxpayers!" exclaimed the woman with the celery. "We are the taxpayers."

"I am a taxpayer," said the fish man. "I even have to pay a tax to sell my fish in the market. Did I ever complain to you that supporting the orphelines was a burden?"

"I pay my taxes too," spoke up an old man who had come to the market looking for a cheap necktie. "House taxes and military taxes and road taxes and dog taxes. Believe me there are plenty of them, so I have some say in this."

Monsieur de Goupil looked helplessly toward Madame
Capet. But she was already retreating with her bicycle. "I
refuse to take the orpheline," she said. "She is dangerous.
She starts revolutions."

"But Madame—" began Monsieur de Goupil.

"Adieu, Monsieur," said Madame Capet, leaping on her
bicycle without looking for a hill. "It is good-bye forever."

And she fled from the mob on her speedy bicycle.

Monsieur de Goupil faced the revolutionists all alone.
"I try to do my best for the orphelines," he pleaded.

"Is it the best thing for them to be adopted against their
will?" asked the woman with the market basket.

"We are taxpayers and we say the orphelines can't be adopted unless they agree to it," said the old man.

Monsieur de Goupil clutched Brigitte's fingers with one hand and pulled his beret down over his perspiring forehead with the other.

He started off with Brigitte. He walked fast, almost dragging her along. The people of Ste. Germaine followed. The policeman followed too. And behind him came the dogs who had recognized their mistresses.

"We will make sure that you take her to the orphanage," said the truck driver.

"And there will be no adoption unless it is agreeable to the children," said the woman with the black shawl.

"From now on we will keep a closer watch on this orphanage," said the woman carrying the bunch of celery.

All the orphelines were peeping through the gate. At sight of Brigitte being pulled along by Monsieur de

Goupil and followed by an angry mob, they began crying lustily.

Madame Flattot looked over their heads. "Please don't be too harsh with the child," she begged Monsieur de Goupil. "She hasn't been well lately. I don't believe she is herself."

Genevieve backed Madame up. "It's the fever," she said. "She's been out of her head with a fever."

"Don't you dare hurt my Brigitte," cried Josine with blazing eyes. She began to punch Monsieur de Goupil with her little fists.

"It is quite all right, children," flustered Monsieur de Goupil, who felt that he had had more than his share of trouble with the orphelines lately. "You shall have a party tonight and tomorrow there will be no school."

As he led Brigitte through the gate, the people stepped back.

"Poor orphelines!" said a woman. "Now they will have a little happiness in their sad lives."

The gate slammed shut. Josine hugged Brigitte. "Who are all those people?" she asked. "Are they our fathers and mothers too?"

Brigitte let go of Monsieur de Goupil's hand and hugged Josine back. "Of course," she answered proudly. "They are France."